# TO BATHE
# A BOA

## by C. IMBIOR KUDRNA

Carolrhoda Books, Inc./Minneapolis

*This book is available in two editions:*
Library binding by Carolrhoda Books, Inc.
Soft cover by First Avenue Editions
241 First Avenue North
Minneapolis, Minnesota 55401


LIBRARY OF CONGRESS CATALOGING-IN-PUBLICATION DATA

Kudrna, C. Imbior (Charlene Imbior)
    To bathe a boa.

    Summary: At bathtime a youngster has to struggle to
get his recalcitrant pet boa into the tub.
    [1. Boa constrictor—Fiction. 2. Snakes as pets—
Fiction. 3. Baths—Fiction. 4. Stories in rhyme]
I. Title.
PZ8.3.K944To   1986              [E]              86-14726
    ISBN 0-87614-306-0 (lib. bdg.)
    ISBN 0-87614-490-3 (pbk.)

            6   7   8   9   10   96   95   94   93   92   91

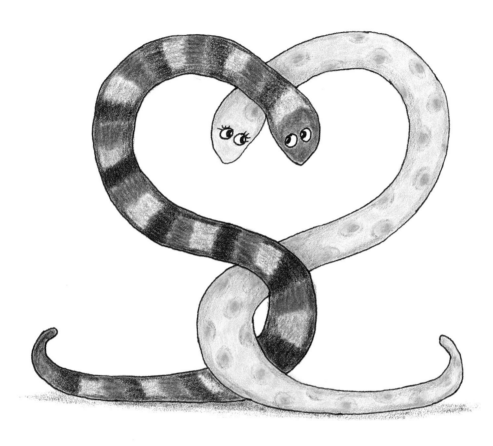

*For Denny, my main squeeze. Love, Charboa*

With soap in hand and water hot,

I called my boa to the spot.

"It's dinnertime," I sweetly lied,

but not a sound did he reply.

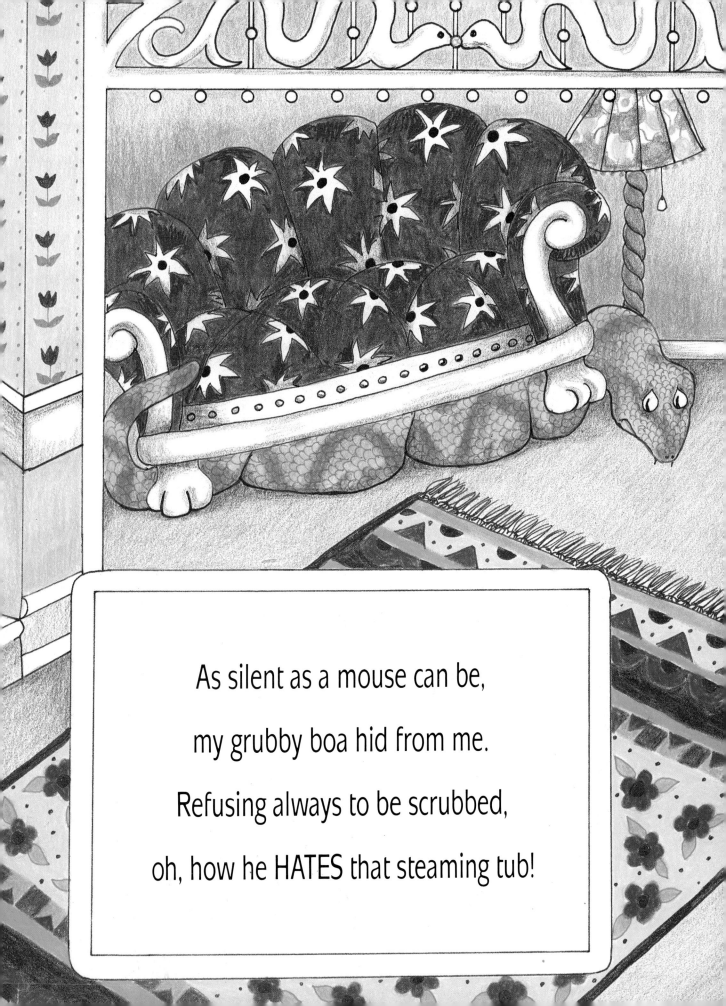

As silent as a mouse can be,

my grubby boa hid from me.

Refusing always to be scrubbed,

oh, how he HATES that steaming tub!

I shook his box of boa chow

and hoped the sound would lure him out.

But he refused to show his face

outside his secret boa place.

Fed up with hide-and-seek type games,

I called my warning as I came.

"Prepare for battle if you must.

This time I vow…it's CLEAN OR BUST!"

I looked inside his boa house

and found he wasn't there....

I peeked into his favorite room

and saw his empty chair....

At last I searched the bedroom,

where I noticed in a bit,

that he'd hidden in the toybox,

(but his tail did not quite fit).

"AHA!" I squealed and grabbed him fast,

but holding him just couldn't last.

For a boa has no greater wrath,

than when he doesn't want a bath!

We tossed and tumbled, fell and rolled.

He slithered and swayed, but I held my hold.

Then with a twist in snakelike style,

he shook me off into a pile.

Back on my feet and chasing fast,

I caught him in a tighter grasp.

This time I knew I had to win,

and get him to that tub…and IN!

Then finally, with bath in view,

I gave a SHOVE…but he did, too.

And tail over feet, boa over limb,

we hit the water—first me, then him.

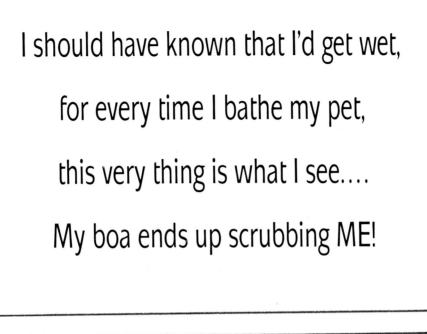

I should have known that I'd get wet,

for every time I bathe my pet,

this very thing is what I see....

My boa ends up scrubbing ME!